Brockworth Library, Moorfield Road,
Brockworth, Gloucester. GL3 4EX
Tel: 01452 863681 Email:
office@brockworthlink.org.uk
www.brockworthlink.org.uk

**Items should be returned to any Gloucestershire County Library on or
before the date stamped below. This book remains the property of the
Brockworth Community Library and can be renewed in person or by
telephone by calling 01452 862 730**

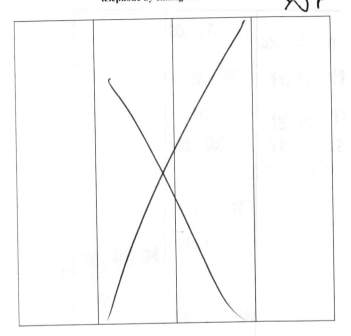

Also in the Definitely Daisy series:

You're a disgrace, Daisy!
Just you wait, Winona!
I'd like a little word, Leonie!
Not now, Nathan!
What's the matter, Maya?

Gloucestershire County Library	
992OO4998 O	
Askews	2 5·0l
JF	£3.50

You must be joking, Jimmy!

Jenny Oldfield

Illustrated by
Lauren Child

*Hodder
Children's
Books*

a division of Hodder Headline Limited

Especially for Joe, Fran and Liz

Text copyright © Jenny Oldfield 2001
Illustrations copyright © Lauren Child 2001

First published in Great Britain in 2001
by Hodder Children's Books

The right of Jenny Oldfield to be identified as the Author of
the work has been asserted by her in accordance with the
Copyright, Designs and Patents Act 1988.

10 9 8 6 5 4 3 2 1

All rights reserved. No part of this publication may be
reproduced, stored in a retrieval system, or transmitted
in any form or by any means without the prior written
permission of the publisher, nor be otherwise circulated
in any form of binding or cover other than that in which
it is published and without a similar condition being imposed
on the subsequent purchaser.

All characters in this publication are fictitious,
and any resemblance to real persons, living or dead,
is purely coincidental.

A Catalogue record for this book is available from
the British Library

ISBN 0 340 78500 4

Printed and bound in Great Britain

Hodder Children's Books
a division of Hodder Headline Ltd
338 Euston Road
London NW1 3BH

One

'A tattoo?' Daisy echoed. She stared hard at her friend, Jimmy Black. 'A real tattoo?'

'Yeah, why not?' Jimmy shrugged. 'Tattoos are cool.'

'B-b-but...!'

'Way to go, Leonie!' Jade, Jared, Kyle and Maya cheered loudly as Leonie picked up her last potato, popped it in her sack, then sprinted for the finish-tape.

'B-b-but...!' Daisy was still spluttering when Leonie burst through the tape ten yards ahead of her nearest rival. 'What's the tattoo of? Where is it? How big?'

Jimmy tossed his head so that his floppy brown hair flipped back from his forehead. He stood up from the grass and set off strolling towards the start of the obstacle race. Weaving in and out of the crowd of kids and parents all gathered on the playing-field for the school sports day, he paused to wait for Daisy.

'I didn't say I'd *got* a tattoo,' he explained. 'What I said was, I *wanted* one!'

'A tattoo?' Winona Jones elbowed her way into their conversation. She joined Jimmy and Daisy dressed in the whitest pair of shorts, the best pressed T-shirt and the most expensive trainers money could buy. 'Oh, puh-lease!' she smirked. 'What a joke!'

'Butt out, Win-oh-na!' Daisy snapped. 'So, Jimmy, why do you want this tattoo?'

'All those children who have been entered for the obstacle race, please take their positions at the start!' Mrs Hunt announced wearily over the loudspeaker. It had been a long, tiring afternoon for the elderly teacher.

At the far end of the course, young Miss Ambler stood ready to record the winners in her diary. Her long, dark blue cotton skirt billowed in the wind, revealing a pair of cheesy-white legs.

'I want a tattoo because Robbie Exley just got one done on his right shoulder blade.' Jimmy came clean with the reason.

'Yeah, but...' Daisy still couldn't put her thoughts into words. 'A *real* tattoo!'

'Take your positions,' Mrs Hunt repeated in a tinny voice.

Jimmy lined up next to Daisy, with Winona on his far side. 'I want a lion roaring, with its mouth wide open,' he whispered earnestly. 'Just like Robbie.'

Super-Rob, the Steelers' ace goal-scorer. Robbie Exley, Jimmy's all-time soccer hero. If Robbie had a tattoo, then that explained everything.

In lane three Winona snorted and shook her blonde head.

'Next thing, you'll be having your hair cropped to a stubble and wearing an ear-stud!' Daisy warned. She didn't think that a lion tattoo would suit shy Jimmy. Nor did she think it would fit on his skinny shoulder-blade. But she decided not to tell him up front in case it hurt his feelings.

'Would Nathan Moss please hurry and line up at the start of the obstacle race!' Mrs Hunt whined over the megaphone. 'Nathan?... Has anyone seen Nathan Moss?'

Meanwhile Bernie King, the school caretaker, stood with a bright green flag raised high over his head, ready to sweep it down to the ground for the start of the final race of the day. Fat Lennox, his asthmatic white bulldog, sat wheezily at his side.

'What's wrong with me having a tattoo?' Jimmy demanded, his face flushing red and growing stubborn.

'Nothing!' Daisy assured him.

Winona snorted and swallowed a giggle.

'...Ah, there you are, Nathan!' Mrs Hunt
sighed, then signalled to Bernie King that
they were ready at last.

Nathan had appeared out of the crowd in
a pair of too-big, borrowed trainers. His wild,
straw-coloured hair stuck up as usual, but he
was minus his taped-up glasses and minus
Legs, his pet spider.

'Jimmy Black says he wants a tattoo!'
Winona sniggered to Nathan.

Nathan blinked back. 'Weird!' he muttered.

'What's weird about it?' Daisy stuck up for
her best friend. 'If Jimmy wants a tattoo like
Robbie Exley's, what's to stop him?'

'Ready!' Bernie roared, flag poised.

'The law,' Nathan pointed out coolly. 'That's
what's to stop him. Jimmy's only nine. He
can't have a tattoo without his parents'
permission!'

The news shocked and dismayed poor
Jimmy. 'Is that true?'

'Yeah, 'course. Didn't you know that?'
Winona sniggered.

'On your marks, get set...!' The King of
Woodbridge Junior roared the commands.
Lennox coughed and wheezed all over
Nathan.

'Is it?' Jimmy whispered to Daisy.

Shoving her untidy mass of long, dark hair
behind her ears, Daisy leaned forward, ready
to dash. Know-all Nathan was always right. 'I
guess so,' she admitted.

'...Go!' Bernie barked.

And twelve reluctant kids sprinted for the
first obstacle while a crowd of so-called
grown-ups screamed blue murder and
egged them on.

'Nathan Moss!' Painstakingly Miss Ambler
noted down the winner, while Daisy, Jimmy
and the rest still struggled through a bright
blue plastic tunnel towards the finish-tape.

Would Daisy's lungs take the strain?
Would she be able to hold her breath in this

underwater cave, grasp the gleaming pearl from the pink depths of the oyster shell, fight her way through the jungle of seaweed, past the tentacles of the humungous octopus and break the surface without gasping for non-existent air? Glug-glug-glug. The bubbles rose, her eyes almost popped out of her head as she fought her way through.

'Second, Winona Jones!' Miss Ambler recorded the runner-up.

Back in the blue tunnel, Daisy elbowed her way past Kyle Peterson.

'Ouch!' Kyle yelped and rolled to one side. 'Help! Daisy Morelli just sat on me. Now I'm stuck!'

Glug-glug! Almost there. The pearl was priceless. It would make Daisy wealthy beyond her wildest dreams...

'Third, Jade Harrison!' Her duty finished, Miss Ambler put her diary on a nearby plastic chair. She ran to rescue Kyle, who, to judge by the muffled yelps and cries, seemed to have collapsed in the tunnel.

Whoosh! Pearl in hand, Daisy burst from the exit and took a great gulp of air.

Miss Ambler dropped on to her hands and knees to peer inside the blue tube. 'Kyle,' she called. 'Where are you? Are you all right?'

'Please Miss, I'm stuck!' came the muffled reply.

Sprinting for the finish-line, Daisy came up alongside Jimmy.

'Who won?' she gasped. Maybe her ears
had been deceiving her when Miss Ambler
had called Nathan's name. Geeky Nathan
couldn't run or climb things to save his life.
Could he?

'Nathan Moss,' Jimmy grunted, his arms
going like pistons as he pounded over the
last ten metres.

'C'mon, Daisy *mia*! R-r-run, run, run, my

bambino!'

Daisy cringed as she heard her dad's lilting voice soar above the rest.

Wow, was this embarrassing. Her dad, Gianni, yelling and drawing attention to her as she came a lame fifth after Jimmy. 'Go home and make pizza!' she muttered to herself. 'Chop onions, make tomato sauce, grate cheese – anything!'

But her dad grabbed her as she crossed the line and gave her one of his big bear-hugs. 'Never mind the winning,' he grinned. 'It's the taking part that counts!'

With a *real* priceless pearl Daisy would buy her mum and dad the biggest pizza restaurant in the world she decided, as she watched Nathan go up to Mrs Hunt to record his winning time.

The Pizza Palazzo would be a *real* palace, not just a little shop on Duke Street. It would be made of pink and white marble, the taps on the sinks would be solid gold...

All around, parents were claiming their kids and carting them off to their cars.

'Well done, dear.'

'...Never mind, don't cry.'

'What happened, Kyle? Did someone deliberately injure you...?'

Quickly Daisy dodged out of her dad's embrace. She slipped away to help Jimmy stack plastic chairs.

'Erm, if anyone would care to stay behind and help us to clear up, we'd be most grateful!' Mrs Hunt whinged through the megaphone.

'Hey!' Jimmy said suddenly. He seized a black book from one of the chairs and opened it. 'This is Rambler-Ambler's diary!'

'Let me see!' Daisy pounced, snatched it from him and read the gold lettering on the cover. Sure enough: WEEK-TO-VIEW DIARY. Inside, on the very first page, above the list of times for sunrise and sunset, she made out the name, Louise Ambler.

'Louise!' Daisy crowed.

'Daisy *mia*, come quick. We have to go home and open the Palazzo. People want pizza!' her dad called from the gate.

'Coming!' she called back. 'Jimmy, did you see this? Boring-Snoring's first name is Louise!'

'Jimmy, Daisy, what are you two up to?' Mrs Hunt had crept up on them unexpectedly, megaphone in hand.

'Nothing!' Jimmy jumped a mile.

Daisy whipped the diary behind her back and assumed an innocent air.

'Hmm.' The teacher looked at them suspiciously. 'Run along home,' she said shortly. 'No, Jimmy, don't argue. And Daisy, have you gone deaf? Didn't you hear your father calling you?'

'B-b-but!' It was Daisy's day for stammering and stuttering. How could she put back Miss Ambler's diary without facing some serious questioning?

("...Daisy Morelli, why were you prying into Miss Ambler's private diary?...Daisy, tut-tut, what are you doing poking your nose into Miss Ambler's personal affairs?...Mr and Mrs Morelli, I'm afraid your daughter has got herself into serious trouble yet again!")

'Go along!' Mrs Hunt threatened, sounding tired and frazzled.

In the distance, Miss Ambler was busy collapsing the long blue tube and folding it up.

'C'mon, Daisy!' Jimmy grunted through gritted teeth.

'B-b-but...!' Oh, this was hopeless.

So Daisy shoved the stupid diary into the back waistband of her shorts, covered it with her T-shirt, then turned and ran for the gate.

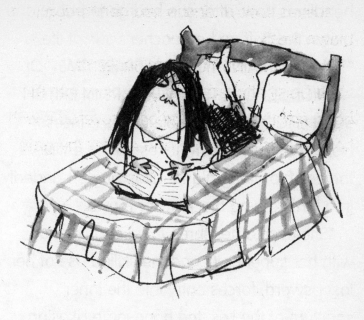

Two

The black book was a doorway into Miss Ambler's life beyond school. An illegal but fascinating glance behind the scenes. And it had fallen into Daisy's ownership almost by accident.

Holding the diary between her hands in the privacy of her own bedroom, Daisy's fingers trembled.

"SCHOOL SHOCKER!" Daisy could see the

headlines now, after she had gone public and blown the gaff on her teacher's secret life. "TEACHER TRAINS TIGERS IN SPARE TIME!" Or, "JUNIOR SCHOOL TEACHER STARS IN BRITISH SCI-FI EPIC!" "Louise Ambler, alias Princess Nola in Asteroid Army, takes on the entire forces of far-flung planet Likos single-handedly in a forthcoming blockbuster movie.

"She overcomes three thousand Likosians with her superior IQ and the skilled use of her laser-sword, forces entry into the inner sanctum of the Los, the handsome Likosian ruler, and finally persuades him through her beauty and her silver-tongued charm to submit to the authority of Queen Tara and her Galactic Guard..." This was *before* Miss Rambler Ambler had switched jobs and become the most boring teacher in the universe, of course.

Miss Boring Snoring. Bad career move, as things turned out, when, if she'd stuck with acting, Louise could have had all Hollywood at her feet.

'Daisy, have you finished your homework?' Her mum called up the stairs.

'Yep,' she lied. In fact, she planned to borrow Leonie's maths book on the way to school tomorrow morning and crib the answers from her stunningly clever and generous friend.

'Supper will be ready in five minutes... Daisy, did you hear me?'

'Uh? What?...OK!' With shaking hands she opened up the diary and turned to the middle pages.

"July 2, Monday – Send off SAT test results. Phone mother. Wash hair in evening." Major let-down. Daisy flicked to the bottom of the next page and tried again.

"July 6, Friday." This would be better. Friday would be Louise's day to go clubbing, meet up with her girlfriends, get drunk and let down her mousy hair.

"Buy new M & S blouse for school (cream, size 12, to go with dark blue skirt).

Dentist's appointment, 4.45pm." And that was

it for that week. Major, major disappointment.

'...Daisy, supper!' Angie Morelli called.

'Coming! Just let me finish my last maths sum!'

'I thought you said you'd done your homework?'

'What? Oh yeah. Sorry. I have. Coming!'

Trying but failing to slip the small black book into her trouser pocket, Daisy hid it instead under her pillow next to beanie babe Herbie and went downstairs without it.

'And this is my own favourite dish: Pizza Gianni!' Daisy's dad charmed the money out of his customers' pockets as Daisy went through the restaurant into the kitchen to find her mum.

'Pizza *al funghi* with crushed garlic – mmm! – fresh herbs and a mountain of *formaggio* all melted to a delicious crispy topping on a deep-pan base!'

'It sounds wonderful!' the young couple sitting at the window table murmured, gazing into each other's eyes over a single red rose.

'Beans-on-cheese-on-toast!' Angie announced the menu for Daisy's own supper. 'On the worktop.' She didn't turn round because she was in the middle of playing aeroplanes with Baby Mia's apple-and-custard pudding.

'*Neeee-aaahhh!*' Angie held the loaded spoon poised eighteen inches above Mia's head. Then she swept her hand down like a jet-fighter, making plane noises.

Mia cooed, gurgled, then opened her mouth just as the spoon dipped by. *Gulp*. The pudding was gone.

'Good girl!' Daisy's mum murmured. 'More?'

Meanwhile, Daisy grabbed her plate. Beans-on-cheese-on-toast was her own favourite dish. No crushed garlic, no fresh herbs to spoil things...

'Don't gobble,' her mum said without looking.

A fork full of beans from the tin plate,

swilled down with strong black coffee, then
saddle up your horse and hit the trail.

This was the cowboy's life...

'Close your mouth while you're eating,'
Angie ordered. Then *'Nee-aagghhh – gulp!'*
Another plane found its target.

'How come Mia can eat with her mouth
wide open?' Daisy protested.

'Don't talk with your mouth full!'

Daisy gave up and scoffed her soggy
toast, jumping up from the table just as her
mum lifted Mia out of her baby-seat and
prepared to take her upstairs to the flat.
Angie sat Mia on her hip and followed
Daisy upstairs, wading into her room after
her through heaps of magazines and
comics which lay strewn across the floor.

'Any stray laundry?' her mum asked,
swooping on the grass-stained shorts at the
foot of Daisy's bed.

Mia enjoyed the roller-coaster ride. 'Goo-
goo-ca-choo!'

'What about your bedclothes?' Angie

demanded. She pounced on the nearest pillow.

There lay Miss Ambler's little black book beside a crushed Herbie hamster. *Disaster!*

'What's that?'

'Nothing!' Daisy leapt on to the bed from the far side of the room. She grabbed the diary before her mum could pick it up, knocking poor Herbie clean on to the floor. ' 'Sprivate!'

'Since when did you start keeping a diary?' Angie asked suspiciously.

Daisy blushed. 'Ages ago. No one can look. 'sprivate!'

'OK, OK! Don't bite my head off. I was only curious.'

Wrestling the pillowcases from the pillows with one hand, Angie got on with her work.

Baby Mia rocked and rolled with the motion. Then she wriggled free from her mum's hip and toddled to pick up Herbie.

'Ah yes, washing-machine for you!' Angie saw the scruffy stuffed hamster and decided he too was for the wash.

'Aw Mum, does he have to?' Daisy fought Mia for possession.

She pulled Herbie's legs while her sister kept strong hold of his head in her podgy fingers. 'He's not even dirty!'

'He's filthy!' Angie decreed.

'But he's already lost one eye in the machine!' Tug-tug-tug.

The truth was, Daisy didn't like to go to sleep without Herbie cuddled up beside her. He was the one who knew all her secrets, the one she planned to read the rest of Miss Ambler's diary to later.

Their mum settled the argument by grabbing Herbie herself.

She whisked the squidgy toy on to the laundry pile, scooped it all up and quickly left the room.

' 'Snot fair!' Daisy yelled.

'Waagh!' Mia cried.

"July 13. Friday." Daisy snuggled between her

clean sheets minus Herbie. She'd taken the
diary into the shower in case anyone came
across it while she was washing her hair.
Now its pages were crinkled and smudged.

Friday the thirteenth! Daisy was
superstitious. Surely something really bad
and exciting must have happened to Miss
Ambler on that day of all days!

"*Lost my grandmother's precious diamond
ring!*" she expected to read. "*Of great
sentimental value. The ring was given to her
by a mysterious gypsy woman who warned
her that if she lost the ring, then she would
be forever cursed!*" Or, "*Was in town with
my friends. Had my Gucci watch stolen from
my wrist as we queued outside Angels. The
police say it's the work of a gang
responsible for a wave of similar snatches in
the city centre. They've asked me to work
with them as a decoy on future cases. Will
discuss it with Mrs Waymann, my
headteacher, before I decide to risk my life
as gangster bait...*" Or even, "*Lost a £20*

note down a drain. Must be my unlucky day!" But no. What Daisy in fact read was four words. "Meeting with bank manager." The real entry was so boring that she practically lost the will to live.

Or at least to stay awake.

"July 14, Saturday – Stayed in. Watched Casualty." Zzzz...

"July 15, Sunday – Stayed in. Sewed sacks for sack-race for Wednesday's sports day." Daisy's head drooped. Boring, boring, boring. Nothing to tell Jimmy except that Miss Rambler-Ambler washed her hair and went to the dentist like everyone else.

Unless, of course, Daisy used a little imagination and made up one or two harmless, juicy details...

Three

'No!'

Yeah, honest!'

'You're kidding me! '

'No, Jimmy, I'm not. Honest. Miss Ambler did belong to a mega-successful girl-band. Cross my heart and hope to die!'

Daisy hid a grin, her fingers firmly crossed behind her back, then paused at the park gates to borrow Leonie's homework. She made Jimmy lean over, so she could use his scrawny back as a flat surface to scribble Leonie's answers into her own dog-eared maths book.

'Hmm!' Kyle Peterson passed by with Winona, limping slightly, and wearing a tight bandage around his left knee. 'Looks to me like someone's copying someone else's work!'

'So?' Leonie challenged. With her glorious halo of curly hair, she was a head taller and twice as tough as weedy Kyle.

Winona tilted her head to one side so that a sweep of blonde curls fell across her shoulder. 'Yeah, Kyle; so what?'

Surprised by Winona's fierce interruption, Kyle backed off then walked on with her towards school. 'So, nothing.'

Leonie grinned. 'That Winona; she's got Kyle knocked into shape, no problem!'

Daisy and the gang were finding that the ex-Mizz Perfect had her uses since she'd decided to smash her goody-goody image.

True, Winona was still hard to take sometimes. There was that shampoo-advert hairstyle for a start. And the poor girl still couldn't avoid being a smug know-all as well as the teacher's number one pet. "Winona dear, could you fetch my handbag? ...Winona, would you run a little errand for me, please?" But basically they now knew where they stood with her.

They were cast-iron certain for instance that she would never let soppy Kyle snitch on Daisy.

'Hurry up!' Jimmy pleaded from beneath Daisy's maths book. His face was turning red with the effort of having to stand in such an awkward, bent position.

'Nearly finished,' she muttered.

Growing bored, Leonie decided to go on ahead. 'See you at school,' she called as she sprang on to a stone wall and ran along the top without faltering. 'Don't mess up my book, OK!'

'This diary...' Jimmy said, returning to the

earlier subject.

'It definitely – like, *definitely* says that Miss Ambler was a member of a girl-band?'

'Yeah, she had a wild youth,' Daisy insisted straight-faced, polishing off the homework and stuffing both books into her jam-packed schoolbag. Then she gave free rein to her imagination. 'The band was called Iced Melon. They played gigs all over the country; all-night raves, summer rock concerts, that kind of thing.'

'You're joking!' Jimmy double double-checked. His dark-grey eyes grew round and wide in his pointed face. 'What did she do? Play drums... or was it keyboard?'

'No. Lead guitar and vocals.' Daisy's mouth quivered at the corners.

Miss Ambler in skin-tight black leather, wailing her way into the Top Twenty. *Sock-it-to-me, sock-it-to-me.*

'Puh!' Jimmy's mouth popped open with a startled explosion of breath. 'So what's she teaching us lot for, then?'

Daisy shrugged, deciding on a diversion through the park which might make them a minute late for school, but which would take them by the duck-pond. 'Y'know how it is,' she told him, skirting the kids' play area. She swung around the pole of a No-Fouling sign to face him. 'Fame and all that stuff. It doesn't last five minutes. Iced Melon had a number one hit five years ago with "Maybe Tomorrow", then that was it.'

'"Maybe Tomorrow"?' Jimmy racked his brains to remember the monster hit. 'Iced Melon?'

'Forget it,' Daisy recommended. She came to the edge of the pond and stopped to look at a family of speckled brown and yellow ducklings paddling their feet and dabbling their beaks in the murky water. 'Because, listen Jim, there was something even more interesting in Ambler's diary!'

'There was?' Jimmy's eyes lit up, ready for Daisy to dish the dirt on the teacher once more.

She nodded. 'This is top-secret, OK? I mean, it only happened last weekend, so probably nobody knows anything about it yet...' Deliberately, Daisy paused. Jimmy was like a fish in a pond, swimming with his mouth open towards the wriggling bait...

'...No way!'
'Who are you trying to kid?'
'You must be joking, Jimmy!'
Jimmy hadn't been able to wait to break

the news about Rambler-Ambler. He mingled
with his friends and listened to their reactions
as the class filed into assembly.

'Ssh!' Mrs Hunt hissed at Jade, Jared and
Maya.

'It's true!' Jimmy insisted. 'Ask Daisy!'

All eyes turned to her. 'Tell you later!' she
mouthed back as she reached her place and
sat cross-legged on the floor.

'Daisy Morelli, I might have known!' With
surprising speed Mrs Hunt leaped from her
seat at the side of the hall. With a swing of
her skirt and a flurry of fawn pleats, she
pounced on Daisy and wagged a finger for
her to come out of the row.

'If there's chattering going on during our
morning worship, I can be sure to find you at
the centre of it!'

Daisy cowered and scowled. She felt like
she'd been mauled by a toothless tiger.

'Don't say another word!' Mrs Hunt
warned, forcing Daisy to stand by her side as
Mrs Waymann the headteacher swept by in

a cloud of perfume.

'I didn't...' Daisy began.

Mrs Hunt savaged her with a look.

So Daisy faked singing and listening, then openly fidgeted her way through the head's boring notices.

'...Winner of the obstacle race: Nathan Moss!' Mrs Waymann announced at last. 'Runner up: Winona Jones!'

The two stood up while the school applauded politely. Only Daisy from her disgraced position saw Legs dozing peacefully in the gap between Nathan's shirt collar and his neck.

Nathan rubbed a hand through his sticky-up hair, then secretly stroked his pet spider, while Winona gave a smug little smile.

'And thank you everyone for helping to make our school sports day such a splendid success!' Mrs Waymann beamed down on her charges, then added an extra notice. 'Now, I'd like a little word with those who kindly stayed behind to help with the clearing up.'

Sixth sense made Jimmy glance quickly and guiltily in Daisy's direction.

She ducked her head, able to guess what was coming next.

The headteacher purred on in a soft, concerned tone of voice.

'Now, if any of you happened across a small black book belonging to Miss Ambler, could you please let a member of staff know where you last saw it?'

Jared, Jade and Maya pressed their lips tight together and stared at the floor.

Leonie slid her neighbour, Jimmy, a curious look.

Winona, Nathan and Kyle felt a small shiver of guilt run along the row.

'The book is important to Miss Ambler,' Mrs Waymann explained, her eyes suddenly darting like an eagle's around the room. No more Mrs Nice Guy. 'Does anyone know anything about it?'

No reply. From Mrs Hunt's side of the hall, Daisy stared straight across at their novice teacher, whose pale face had flushed a bright shade of pink.

There was a long, awkward silence.

'Very well. Dismissed.' Mrs Waymann frowned in disappointment as she left the platform.

And it seemed to Daisy that the head's passing glance caught her and cut through her like a knife.

* * *

'Honest, Jimmy; I swear Waymann knows who took the diary!' she whispered at playtime later that morning.

'You didn't *take* it, exactly!' he hissed back.

She darted a narrow look at him, then corrected his slip of the tongue. '*We* didn't take it!'

'OK, *we* didn't take it. It happened by mistake. But what are you gonna do now?'

'What are we gonna do now? Hmm.'

Problem. There was the diary, tucked under her mattress at home, safe from prying eyes. Meanwhile, here at school, Waymann would mount an internal investigation to recover it.

'...So, Jade Harrison, do you swear that you have nothing whatsoever to do with the disappearance of the vital document?'

Jade, sweating and trembling, would mumble her reply. 'No, miss.'

Curiously, Mrs Waymann suddenly seemed to be sporting a trim military moustache and wearing a uniform with brass buttons and gold shoulder pads. 'Speak up, girl! If you personally had nothing to do with it, can you at least tell me who did?'

Soldiers' boots would be marching up and down the dingy corridor outside, one-two, one-two! Rifles would click in the bare, grey playground outside as they lined up the next victim against this very, self-same concrete wall...

'We have to work out a way of bringing the

diary back without anyone knowing it was
us,' Daisy decided.

'Yeah, and fast,' Jimmy insisted. He tugged
at the short sleeves of his blue football shirt,
pulling them down over his skinny elbows
until his entire arms disappeared.

'What are you doing? Why aren't you
playing football?'

Winona broke in on Daisy and Jimmy's
quiet conversation in the corner of the
playground.

'Go away, Winona!' Jimmy snapped.

She took no notice. 'And what's this weird stuff I just heard about Miss Ambler?' she said suspiciously.

'What weird stuff?' Daisy countered.

Jared appeared out of nowhere. 'You know!' He winked and grinned. 'You're the ones who told us!'

'About Ambler's love-life!' Maya added, peering out earnestly from behind Jared.

'Miss Ambler's in lu-u-urve!' Jade giggled. She'd shown up as suddenly as the rest. Hot gossip in the far corner, behind the bike-shed. Gossip-alert, gossip-alert!

'Yeah, but this is a joke, isn't it?' Winona turned on Jimmy and cornered him good and proper. 'From what I hear, it can't possibly be true!'

'Why not?'

'It can't be. I mean, Miss Ambler and...' Infected by Jade's snorting, spluttering laughter, Winona too began to smile.

'It's true!' Jimmy said hotly. He ducked

under Winona's arm and gained the upper hand. Turning back, he shot his hands out from his sleeves and placed them squarely on his hips.

'It was in her diary entry for last Saturday, the fourteenth of July!'

Daisy jumped forward to step smartly on Jimmy's toes. Too late.

Winona stopped giggling and let her mouth fall open. 'What diary? Is that the black book Waymann was on about?'

He nodded. 'Saturday the fourteenth!' Poor, football-mad Jimmy wanted desperately to believe. And he needed to convince the whole school that what Daisy had told him was true. So he turned to her with a pleading look.

'So?' Winona demanded.

Daisy took a deep breath. There was nothing for it; she was in a mess but she would just have to tough this one out. 'So, it's true,' she said. 'Miss Ambler – er, Louise – is in lurve with Jimmy's hero and the Steelers' superstar...'

'N-n-no...!' Winona stammered.

'Right! Our very own teacher here at Woodbridge Junior is going out with Robbie Exley!'

Four

Before Winona's jaw hit the tarmac in surprise, Daisy obligingly filled in the details.

'Of course, it's early days. They only became an item last Saturday. They met at Angel's nightclub and it was love at first sight.'

'Yeah, yeah!' Winona scoffed.

'It's true!' Jimmy insisted.

Daisy went on. 'Reading between the lines

of Louise's secret diary, I would say it's definitely the real thing!'

By this time, Jade and Jared's sneering smiles were starting to fade. Either Daisy was putting on an Oscar-winning performance, or the story was true. Frown marks formed between their eyes, while Daisy went blithely on.

'LURVE, LURVE, LURVE!' she sang, waltzing Winona around the playground. 'Miss Ambler and Robbie Exley. They're gonna get married and have baby footballers. We'll be old enough by then to babysit, and Jimmy will be able to coach all the young Exleys to become great soccer players like their dad!'

Jimmy's eyes lit up. 'Yeah!' he sighed.

'Hmm.' Winona screwed up her mouth. 'Well. I don't believe a word you say.'

'Who cares what you think?' Jimmy jumped in. Boy, did he want his super-hero to be going out with their teacher! 'You didn't even know that Miss Ambler was lead-singer in a girl-band before she was a teacher, so there!'

While Winona's jaw dropped another mile, Daisy edged towards Jimmy. 'Don't push it!' she advised.

In the background, Jade and Jared smiled nervously, waiting to see which way the argument would go.

'Now I *know* you're joking!' Hands on hips, Winona spoke in a sing-song, you-can't-fool-me voice. 'Jimmy Black, if you think for a nano-second that I'm gonna believe that...!'

'Yeah!' Jared said, slowly making up his own mind. 'No way!'

Daisy gritted her teeth. This wasn't going well.

'Anyway, I read in my mum's magazine that Robbie Exley's girlfriend is a supermodel called Ingrid,' Jade added.

'That was last week, not this week!' Daisy argued weakly.

'This week he's going out with Ambler!'

Jade and Jared came to join Winona, flanking her on either side. In the distance, Miss Ambler herself came out of the main entrance to ring the handbell which would bring everyone back into school for lessons.

Saved by the bell! Daisy thought with a sigh of relief. She and Jimmy made as if to set off across the playground.

But the other three stood firmly in their way.

'OK, so prove it!' Winona challenged with a toss of her golden head and a flash of her clear grey eyes.

Daisy sidestepped uncertainly. Jimmy stuck out his chin.

'Yeah!' Jade and Jared echoed. 'Prove it!'

'What are we gonna do?' Jimmy asked Daisy on the way home from school that evening.

Daisy had spent the day quietly observing Miss Ambler.

Miss Ambler handing back the maths homework: 'Well done, Leonie. Well done, Nathan. You too, Winona.' *Smack*! Daisy's book had been slammed down hard on her desk. 'Daisy Morelli, I've never seen such a disgraceful mess in all my life. It looks like Nathan's spider has stepped in some ink and crawled all over the page!'

Wise Daisy had offered no defence. She'd even deliberately miscopied a couple of Leonie's answers to put Ambler off the scent. Full marks and impeccable presentation would've looked suspicious, she knew.

Then Miss Ambler teaching music in the afternoon. *Doh-re-mi.*

Doh-doh-doh! One thing was for sure, Rambler-Ambler's voice was as flat as a pancake. Daisy caught Winona's sneering glance. Like, yeah; lead singer with Iced Melon – not!

And Ambler giving them a talk about school uniform. *Zzzzz*!

'How we look is important. We must be neat and tidy so that we can be a credit to the school when visitors come. Our shirts must be washed and ironed every day, Daisy. We should wear our ties neatly knotted, like Kyle. We should NOT wear our football kit in school, twenty-four hours a day, seven days a week, should we, Jimmy?'

Zzzzzzzz! Daisy had taken the chance to study Miss Boring-Snoring more closely. Her face was round and pale as a Wensleydale cheese, her brown hair long and wispy. And her fashion sense was truly awful: crumpled dark blue skirt, the famous M & S size 12 cream blouse, shapeless and buttoned up to the neck. Flat, black, sensible sandals...

Daisy herself was no fashion victim, but even *she* could see that there was nothing about the teacher's appearance that would attract the attention of someone like Robbie Exley.

* * *

'I think we should let the whole thing just drop,' she told Jimmy as they stopped on the windy pavement outside his door on Duke

Street later that afternoon. 'If we don't mention the Robbie Exley-Miss Ambler thing any more, then Winona and the others will forget it by the weekend.'

Jimmy sniffed, and scuffed the toe of his trainer against the doorstep of Car World. Inside the shop, his dad was stacking aerosol cans into a paint rack, whistling cheerfully as he worked. 'I don't wanna forget it,' he muttered. 'I wanna prove that we're telling the truth.'

Daisy swallowed hard. She ummed and aahed for a while, considering whether or not to break things gently. Like, "Sorry, Jimmy, I made it all up!" No, that wouldn't work. How about, "Actually, Jim, I just read another extract from the diary and it says that Robbie finished with Louise on Tuesday night."? Better. That might work.

'I thought of one way we could prove it,' he insisted. 'Then the whole school would know I wasn't joking.'

'Er, listen...' Daisy began.

'No, honest; this is a good idea.' Jimmy was convinced that his plan would work. 'What you have to do is take the diary into school tomorrow. You pretend you just found it in a corner of the cloakroom or something. You take it to Ambler and say the page fell open at the part where it tells you about the nightclub and Robbie Exley. Then you ask her

a favour, which she'll do, even if it is her un-
favouritist pupil who's asking, because she's
so grateful to have her diary back...'

As he paused for breath at last, Daisy was
able to interrupt.

'And what favour do I ask Miss Ambler
for?' she queried.

'Well, this is the good bit!' Jimmy gabbled
on, his eyes round with excitement. Standing
in front of the shiny window with giant, neon
stickers anouncing special offers on fast-wax
and anti-freeze, he looked small and innocent.
'You ask Ambler for Robbie's autograph!'

Daisy took a deep breath, hoiked her hair
back behind her shoulders and stuffed it
inside her shirt collar to stop it blowing in the
breeze. 'Right,' she nodded.

'Ambler does what you ask and gives you
the signature. That's proof, see. It shows we
weren't joking after all!'

Jimmy could twist the knife in when he
wanted to.

'Y'see, Herbie; there was this time, ages ago, when Jim and me got to meet Kevin Crowe, the Steelers' manager. Never mind how. I probably told you at the time, but you've forgotten.'

Snuggled in bed beside her, smelling of

washing-powder and fresh air, the stuffed hamster kept his one eye firmly on Daisy.

Daisy sighed at the memory of the golden moment. 'Kevin introduced us to Robbie Exley. We actually met him in person. And Robbie signed the back of my T-shirt.'

What's that got to do with the current mess you've got yourself into? Herbie's eye winked in the lamplight as if he was asking Daisy a hard question.

'So, I actually had Robbie's autograph, see. But it was written on my T-shirt. And Mum saw it the moment I walked through the door. Well, you know what she's like about throwing stuff in the washing machine...'

I sure do, the squidgy, much-spin-dried hamster seemed to agree.

'Before I could stop her, she'd hauled my clothes off my back and stuck them in the machine on hot-wash. Result: no more autograph. It had faded to nothing. Jimmy nearly went crazy. I had to say sorry hundreds of times before he let it drop.'

Jimmy's soccer-crazy, Herbie reminded her. *To him, Robbie Exley is a footballing god.*

'I know it. So, anyway, today when he had this idea about asking Ambler for Robbie's autograph, he reminded me of how I'd gone and lost it in the washing-machine once before. That cut pretty deep, bringing that thing up all over again...'

Which just shows you how much it matters to him. The wise, one-eyed rodent looked deep into Daisy's eyes.

Daisy switched off the light, then turned over in bed, away from Herbie's glassy stare. 'That's just it. I couldn't bear to let him down a second time.'

So?

'So, I said, OK, I'd do it.'

Oh, Daisy!

'I know; stupid, huh? no need to rub it in.'

That's another fine mess you've gotten yourself into.

'Yeah, OK, Herbie. I said lay off, OK!'

With the curtains drawn but the late evening light still filtering through, Daisy knew she was a million miles away from being able to go to sleep. She tossed and turned, rolled into Herbie, still squatting on her pillow, said sorry, moved him to a safe place on her bedside table, then sighed.

'How on earth am I going to do it?' she
wondered out loud. 'I mean, think of how
mega-embarrassing it's gonna be... and
what about poor Jimmy?'

Silence from the golden hamster.

Outside the window, a lorry trundled along
Duke Street, followed by a motorbike roaring
by – *WRROAaaghhh* – *screeeech* –
meeyaAAAGHH!

Daisy shot up in bed. 'Got it!' she cried.
'First thing tomorrow morning, I'll ask Leonie!'

Five

Daisy knew for a fact that Leonie Flowers
would understand.

Offer Leonie something naughty and
nasty and she would leap on it in a flash.
Give her a trick to play, a grown-up to fool,
and she was sure to act it out to
perfection.

Yet Leonie looked as if butter wouldn't
melt, so she never got caught. With her halo

of dark curly hair, she was sweet but not *too* sweet. She seemed helpful without being a goody-goody, clever without a trace of geekiness.

That was why everyone in the world wanted to be best friends with Leonie. And that was the reason why Daisy went to her first thing on Friday to enlist her help.

'This is between you and me, OK?' Daisy insisted.

She'd collared Leonie in the school corridor, between English and P.E.

'Cross my heart,' Leonie swore.

'The main thing is, don't breathe a word to Jimmy.'

Leonie nodded. 'Is it about Ambler's diary?'

'Kind of.' One of Daisy's problems was still how to return the stupid, boring thing to its rightful owner. She'd read through to the last entry, desperately searching for a juicy bit of information that was true, but found nothing. Big fat zero. Miss Ambler's life was DULL, DULL, DULL.

SNOOZEVILLE.

So she'd stuffed the diary into the bottom of her schoolbag and now carried it guiltily with her everywhere she went.

'How are you on forging people's signatures?' she asked Leonie in a casual, off-hand way.

Leonie tilted her head to one side. 'Pretty good.'

'Move along, Daisy Morelli!' Mrs Waymann crossed the entrance hallway in a scented cloud which wafted down the corridor along with her cross-sounding voice. 'Why aren't you changed into your P.E. things like Leonie?'

So Daisy moved along, fishing her trainers out of her bag as they went. 'Whose signatures are you best at?' she inquired.

'Well, Mum and Dad's, obviously,' Leonie admitted. 'And my sister Ariella's, but that's not so good because I don't practise...'

Huff-huff-huff!

Distracted, Daisy looked down to see
horrid Lennox wheezing and panting
down the corridor after them. The fat white
dog came padding right up to her schoolbag and sniffed hard at her trainers. *Huff-
huff.*

'Gerroff, Lennox!' She swung her bag out
of reach, managing in her clumsy hurry to tip
every item on to the floor.

Splat went an uneaten satsuma from
Monday's packed lunch.

Skid went her plastic pencil-case right
down the corridor.

Lennox pounced, gnashed the squashed
fruit between his drooling chops, tasted it,
then spat it back out.

And *flutter-flutter* went Miss Ambler's
private diary, last to tip out of the bag and hit
the floor.

Snarl-grab! Lennox seized the battered,
spattered book.

'Le'go, Lennox!' Daisy wailed.

The bulldog set off at a slow, bow-legged trot down the corridor towards the entrance.

'Lennox, come back!' Daisy's heart thumped. Her mouth went dry as she saw Bernie King's figure loom large in the main doorway.

'Leave this to me!' Leonie murmured, setting off after the dog. Her long legs easily overtook him before he reached the caretaker and she'd already worked out a foolproof plan.

'Hey, Lennox!' she said coolly, leaning over him with both empty hands hidden behind her back. 'Doggy-choc. Which hand?'

Dumb Lennox was fooled by the promise of food. As his saggy eyes looked up at Leonie's bright, eager face, his jaw slackened and he dropped the diary.

Pant-pant-loll-loll. Doggy-choc. Drool.

Leonie stooped with a grin to pick up the book, which she quickly hid behind her back as Bernie King stomped down the corridor.

Luckily the caretaker was too bent on persecuting Daisy to notice. 'You again!' he hollered as she scrabbled to pick up her pencils and felt-tips. He stared down with disgust at the squashed satsuma which his dog's teeth had mashed. 'I might have known! If there's one person in this school always leaving me a mess to clear up, it's definitely you, Daisy Morelli!'

'So, how about it?' Daisy gasped at Leonie.

They were playing a game of pirates during P.E., an end-of-term 'treat' which Miss Ambler had forced on the whole class.

They were in the hall with the equipment set out. Foam mats were scattered across the floor between wooden benches and boxes. The overhead beams were lowered and long ropes swung out across the middle of the room. And the aim was for the teams of pirates to cross from one side to the other without being tagged and without setting foot on the floor.

'How about what?' Leonie replied. She'd landed on Daisy's mat with a graceful leap from the end of a swinging rope.

'Forging a signature for me.' Daisy took up from where they'd left off after the Lennox incident.

'Whose?'

'Robbie Exley's!' Daisy hissed.

'...You're tagged, Daisy!' Kyle yelled at her from a bench ten feet away. 'I got you. You have to go back to the start!'

Daisy raised her eyebrows and deliberately turned her back.

'Miss, Daisy's cheating!' Kyle called to the teacher, but Jimmy landed on his bench and tagged him so hard that he fell off the bench and drowned in the sea.

'Avast!' Jimmy cried, picturing himself in eye-patch and wooden leg. "C'mon, me hearties, let's stab the landlubbers through the vitals, aaargh!'

'Let me get this straight.' Leonie frowned at Daisy while pirates swarmed all around. 'You want me to forge Robbie Exley's signature so that you can give it to Jimmy and he can show it as proof that Miss Ambler really is going out with his hero?'

Daisy nodded eagerly. 'You got it!'

'No way.' Leonie shook her head.

'Why not?' Had she heard right? Had Leonie just refused to help? How could this be?

Behind, above and to each side, pirates' blood-curdling yells drowned out the subject of their frantic conversation.

'Take that, you swine!'

'Aagh! Splash! Help, I can't swim!'

'...Because,' Leonie hissed back, 'I don't think it'll work!'

'Of course it'll work!' Daisy insisted. 'You forge the signature to look exactly like the real thing, then everyone's happy.'

'Unless someone like brainbox Nathan over there works it out and tells,' Leonie pointed out. 'You know what he's like in SATs tests, getting absolutely everything right?'

'Yeah.' Daisy had to admit that Nathan had a computer for a brain. She could feel her one and only plan slipping from her grasp as Leonie got ready to spring from the mat on to the high beam and swing to the safety of their own ship.

'So?'

'So something like a forged...'

'Sshh!' Daisy begged, sneaking a look around the hall.

'...signature isn't gonna fool Nathan

for a single second.'

So, you're under pressure. Herbie looked calmly out from the top of Daisy's schoolbag. P.E. had finished. The school day had moved on. He fixed her with his one glass eye. *This is a science lesson, isn't it? So, be scientific!*

Make a list! Daisy told herself while Miss Ambler demonstrated the way some white stuff turned blue when you heated it on a bunsen burner. After all, a list was scientific:

1. Write to Robbie Exley directly, asking for his signature. (Nope. Robbie must have hundreds of requests just like that. It would take ages for him to get round to sending Daisy what she needed.)

So she crossed out the first idea on the list.

2. Tell Jimmy that Miss Ambler got Robbie's autograph for you, but that fat Lennox came along and ate it while she wasn't looking. (Hmm. How likely was that? Probably about 4 out of 10. Not good.)

3. Say sorry to Jimmy, but the teacher

refused the favour. She said she couldn't possibly take advantage of the fact that she was going out with a famous footballer just to satisfy a pupil's whim. (Better. 6 out of 10. But they would still end up with Nathan, Winona, Kyle etc ripping them to shreds for failing to prove that the story was true.)

Daisy sat, pen poised, chewing the plastic end.

Bubble-bubble-crackle-pop! The white stuff on the front bench turned blue. It let off a whiff of foul-smelling smoke.

4. Tell Jimmy that Robbie blistered his writing hand while conducting a chemical experiment, so he couldn't sign any autographs in the foreseeable future... (Pathetic. Not even worth writing down.)

Daisy nibbled her pen and pondered.

A nearby whisper from Winona into Nathan's ear made her look up.

'Go ahead, Nathan,' Winona urged, a wicked glint in her eye.

'See what she does!'

Nathan took off his glasses to polish them in a bored way.

Rub-rub in tiny circles with the end of his tie.

'I dare you!' Winona hissed, giggling in the direction of Jade and Jared. 'All you have to say is, "Please Miss, how do you cope with the pressure of having a famous boyfriend?"'

No! Daisy almost yelped the little word out loud. She sat on the edge of her stool as she realised that Winona and Nathan were about to call her bluff.

'Stop, fidgeting, Daisy!' Miss Ambler complained without even bothering to look up from her experiment. Her face was flushed with the success of having turned the white powder bright blue.

'Go on, Nathan!' Winona whispered. 'It'll be a laugh!'

'Uh-hum!' Nathan put on his glasses and cleared his throat.

He glanced sideways at Daisy, then at Jimmy sitting two rows in front.

'Yes, Nathan, what is it?' Miss Ambler inquired sweetly, raising her plastic goggles and obviously expecting a difficult science question from her star pupil.

Oh no! This was it! Daisy froze on the edge of her seat.

Exposure. Embarrassment. Shame.

'Please Miss,' Nathan began, his hair sticking up wildly as if he was connected to an electric current. Legs crawled slowly out of the cuff of his shirt sleeve and wandered idly over the chemical formula that Nathan had scribbled in biro on the back of his hand. 'Winona wants to know what it's like going out with a famous boyfriend.'

Six

'Miss, I don't...! Miss, I didn't...!' Winona tried to protest.

Daisy squirmed down behind her desk, doing her best to vanish.

Jimmy's shiny face eagerly awaited Miss Ambler's answer.

Nathan sat with a smug grin, not looking at anyone and softly stroking Legs.

The teacher looked for a moment as if she

hadn't heard the question. Then, when she realised what Nathan had said, she blushed bright scarlet. 'Nathan, I'm going to pretend that I didn't hear that,' she replied sternly, fixing her goggles back over her eyes and poking about amongst the cindery remains of the blue crystals.

Nathan shrugged then popped Legs into his jam-jar, ready for the end-of-school bell.

Daisy breathed again. At least Miss Ambler's answer hadn't exposed the trick she'd been playing on Jimmy.

But of course the teacher, being a teacher, wasn't prepared to let the subject drop.

'Really, Winona, I'm surprised at you,' Rambler-Ambler grumbled as she gave orders for the pupils to pack their bags. 'I didn't expect you of all people to be involved in such silly stories.'

It was Winona's turn to squirm and blush. But she knew better than to lie and worm her way out. 'Sorry, Miss Ambler.'

'I should think so too.' Casting aside her

goggles, the teacher marched purposefully up and down the aisles between the desks. 'What goes on in my private life is my own business, and don't let anyone here suppose otherwise.'

Yeah, bank managers and dentists, blouses

and schoolwork; that's all that goes on in Boring-Snoring's private life, Daisy sighed.

'Which brings me to the subject of my missing diary,' Ambler continued, stopping by chance right beside Daisy's desk.

Diary-in-bag. Bag-under-desk. Danger! Danger! Daisy grew hot all over.

The judge sat at his high bench, weighed down by his long white wig. His eyelids were hooded, his nose hooked like a bird of

prey's. He fixed his piercing eye on the accused.

'Daisy Morelli, do you continue to deny the charge?'

In the dock, Daisy rattled her leg-irons. Pale and dirty after three months in the dungeon, still

she kept her head high and stared back at her accuser. 'I'm innocent, your majesty, your – er – worship. I never went near no stupid diary!'

The shrivelled old man on the podium dismissed her plea.

'Guilty!' he cackled, banging a wooden hammer on his bench.

'That missing book contains a lot of important information,' Miss Ambler went on, her X-ray gaze seemingly fixed on Daisy's schoolbag. 'There are telephone numbers, appointments and addresses which I can't manage without.'

Mega-cringe! Daisy ducked her head so that her neck disappeared into her hunched shoulders.

'Awright, yer honour, it's a fair cop. But it ain't an 'angin' offence, no way!'

'Take her down to the gallows!' the judge snapped. 'Next!'

Miss Ambler stared at Daisy's bag, then

sighed. 'So please, if anyone does happen to come across my diary, be sure to return it to me as soon as possible.'

'Close!' Jimmy admitted, trotting down the left wing to pick up the ball and take a throw-in. He and Daisy had met up in the park that morning; a soggy Saturday, three days before the end of term. And they'd just been recalling the close call of the previous day.

'I really thought I'd had it!' Daisy confessed.

Saturday meant digging your favourite old T-shirt out of the bottom of the laundry basket, slinging on a pair of shorts and trainers and beating a hasty retreat out of the house before your mum could collar you to look after Mia, or your dad could grab you to mix pizza-dough... 'I mean, I could've sworn Ambler could see right through my bag; X-ray eyes – *zzzing*!'

Jimmy raised the ball over his head and aimed down the makeshift pitch. 'You gotta give the diary back!' he insisted.

'I know.' Daisy sped down the centre to collect the throw-in. She dribbled the ball daintily over the rough turf.

"Daisy, Daisy, give us our answer, do!" The crowd roared her on, adapting an ancient popular song. "We're half-crazy, all for the love of you...!"

'I'm just waiting for my chance to put it back on Ambler's desk without being seen.'

Jimmy streaked like a whippet from the sideline towards the goal. He received a pass from Daisy and dribbled on. 'Better make it quick,' he advised. 'We've only got three days of school left.'

Jimmy looked up at the goal (two spare trainers neatly placed on the grass), aimed and shot. His ace left foot found the spot. "Goal!" the fans screamed. 'Yee-eeesss!!!" Daisy watched Jimmy sprawl to the ground, flip up again and raise both arms to the invisible crowd. She joined him in a victory trot around the empty field. 'What did you do with the ball?' she asked, once the excitement had died down.

'Nothing. It landed in the bottom of the hedge.'

So they trotted behind the goal to search, only to be interrupted by the familiar, breathy snarl of Lennox, the school caretaker's dog.

'Uh-oh!' Daisy muttered. It was never a good thing to meet up with Lennox.

'Here, boy!' Bernie King's voice called from the path beyond the spiky hawthorn hedge.

Ignoring his lord and master, Lennox found Jimmy's ball and promptly sank his fangs into it.

Hiss! Daisy and Jimmy watched in dismay as the dog's teeth punctured their football.

'Hey!' Jimmy cried, about to wrestle with the wheezy bulldog.

Daisy pulled him back. 'What's the point? The ball's useless.'

Ducking through a gap in the hedge, they glowered at Lennox, who by this time had waddled off with the ruined ball and dropped it at his owner's size eleven feet.

'Tutt-ttt!' Bernie shook his head and looked at Daisy as if it was all her fault. Like, *Can't a man walk his dog without some brainless twerp kicking a ball in our direction?* 'Now, if you want to know about a kid with *real* footballing talent, you should meet my nephew, William,' he began.

William-this. William-that.

For five whole minutes King blocked the path with his broad figure and went on and on about the miraculous soccer talent of his brother's son.

'William King. He's Barry's boy. You might've heard of him?'

'Nope,' Daisy replied, determined not to listen. All she wanted to do was to retrieve their mashed ball and get out of the drizzling rain that had begun to fall.

'Kevin Crowe just signed him up for the Steelers' youth squad. It was in all the newspapers. He's only seventeen years old, yet they're calling William the best goalkeeping prospect England has had since Gordon Banks in '66.'

'That's fantastic!' Jimmy gasped, utterly impressed by the idea of Bernie's nephew rubbing shoulders with the stars.

'Does he train with the first team players?'

King nodded proudly. 'Yeah, our William's hobnobbing with the likes of Hans Kohl and Pedro Martinez.'

'Robbie Exley?' Jimmy added hopefully.

'C'mon, Jim, let's go!' Daisy tugged at the sleeve of her friend's football shirt, uneasy at the turn of the conversation.

But Jimmy was talking about his one and only passion. He dug in his heels and waited for a reply.

The off-duty caretaker took out a yellow, rolled-up kagoul and struggled into it. Then he nodded again. 'As a matter of fact, Robbie Exley and his girlfriend took our William out clubbing last weekend.'

'Wow!' Jimmy sighed. 'How about that for a coincidence? Last weekend was the first date for Robbie and ...*ouch!*'

Pretending to dive for the flattened ball which Lennox had slobbered all over and finally dropped, Daisy cannoned into Jimmy and stopped him mid-sentence.

Bernie King didn't notice. He just went on boasting about his precious nephew. 'Yes,' he nodded, spraying raindrops from the hood of his kagoul. 'Robbie and Ingrid took our William to Angels nightclub in the centre of town.'

Daisy groaned and sighed.

'Ingrid?' Jimmy interrupted with a puzzled frown. 'Ingrid who?'

'Oh, Ingrid whatsits...' King struggled to remember. 'You know, that blonde supermodel from Sweden. She and Robbie have been seeing each other for the past six months.'

'You made the whole thing up!' Jimmy's accusation rang across the rainy park.

He and Daisy had left Bernie King and Lennox to the rest of their damp walk and ducked back through the hedge.

Now he turned to face her with a look of shocked realisation.

'You lied to me, Daisy. Miss Ambler isn't Robbie Exley's girlfriend at all. She probably doesn't even *know* him!'

Daisy hung her head. The soaking rain had plastered her hair to her face. She shivered inside her wet T-shirt.

'Does she?' Jimmy insisted.

'No.'

He was pale with anger. 'And that means you can't get Robbie's autograph either, can you?'

'No,' she whispered again. She'd let down her best friend, made a fool of him and turned him against her.

Taking a deep breath, he grabbed the deflated ball from her, tucked it under his arm and got ready to sprint off. 'Just you wait, Daisy Morelli!' he yelled at her. 'I mean it; just you wait and see!'

Seven

'Why so gloomy, Daisy *mia*; just like this 'orrible English weather?' Gianni had asked.

All Saturday and Sunday she'd gone around the flat and restaurant with a long face.

'What happened to Jimmy today?' Angie had inquired.

'Mum, that's the fourth time you've asked me,' Daisy had snapped back. 'I don't have to do *everything* with him, do I?'

Even Herbie posed awkward questions. *You know this is all your fault, don't you, Daisy? If you hadn't made up the diary entries in the first place, none of this would have happened.*

Daisy shoved the hamster down to the bottom of her bag as she got ready for school on the Monday morning. *Oh, and by the way; about this diary...* She'd velcroed the bag tight shut to stop him from finishing.

And what had Jimmy meant by yelling 'Just you wait!' at her across the rain-soaked pitch? The problem filled her head as she trudged towards Woodbridge Road.

Did he mean, for instance, that he would never speak to her again? Or that he would find a more sneaky way of getting his own back?

What if, just for example, Jimmy decided to drop Daisy in it over Ambler's diary?

She felt a jolt in her chest as her heart missed a beat. Then she picked up her pace to arrive at school before Jimmy did.

She would have to plead with him, go down on her knees and beg him not to tell. (*I wouldn't blame him if he did*, Herbie grunted from the depths of her bag.) 'Hey, Daisy!' Jade called as she sped through the big iron gates.

Daisy waved and ran on. 'Have you seen Jimmy?' she gasped at Jared, who stood on the top step under the main entrance.

'No, he's not here yet,' he told her. 'He was still having his breakfast when I called at his house.'

'Thank heavens!' Daisy relaxed and collapsed on to the step, dumping her bag beside her.

Nathan, who had sloped silently up the steps after her, had his head in a different universe as usual. Probably the world of black holes and other space mysteries which defied the laws of physics. Anyway, he tripped over Daisy's bag and sent Legs spiralling on an invisible thread towards the floor.

'Daisy Morelli, pick up that bag before someone breaks a leg!' Mrs Gloom-and-Doom Hunt wailed from inside the building.

'Here comes Jimmy now,' Jared warned from his lookout point.

'He's got Leonie, Winona and Kyle with him. And he's waving a piece of paper in their faces. What's going on?'

Already on her feet, Daisy followed Jared across the playground. She noticed that Jimmy wore a grin spreading from ear to ear, without a trace of the shock he'd displayed when she'd confessed the rotten Miss Ambler-Robbie Exley trick to him.

'Talk about lucky!' Leonie sighed, grabbing the paper from Jimmy and reading a long list of names. 'Wow, Jimmy, this is totally A-MAZING!'

'What is?' Daisy pestered, pushing in between Leonie and Jimmy. The list looked like signatures; about a dozen names scrawled haphazardly down the page. 'Jimmy, what is it?'

'Nothing!' he retorted, staring down his snub-nose at her.

He grabbed the paper back from Leonie before Daisy had chance to read it.

'A-MAZING!' Winona echoed with an admiring sigh. She turned to Daisy. 'Jimmy only went and got Robbie Exley's autograph like he said!'

'What...? How...?' Daisy stuttered.

Jimmy flashed her a Cheshire-cat grin, cheesy and mysterious.

'I asked Miss Ambler, like we planned!' he said innocently.

Liar! Daisy shot back a vicious look. But she couldn't breathe a word out loud. (*Well, you lied to him first*, old Herbie remarked from her bag on the top step.) 'AND he's got autographs from the entire first team!' Kyle added. 'Hans Kohl... Pedro Martinez, plus Kevin Crowe!'

'Never, Jimmy! You must be joking!' Daisy gasped. She felt her legs go weak. Surely he couldn't have... wouldn't have...no, definitely not!

But then again, how else could Jimmy have the set of twelve signatures if he hadn't sat and faked the whole blooming lot?

'And today, Class 5A, we're in for a big surprise!' Miss Ambler stood at the front of the room and promised the group a special end of term treat.

No, I can't take any more surprises! Daisy groaned inwardly.

First, there was Jimmy and his set of "autographs". Huh, what a way to get his own back; forging all twelve signatures! Daisy had sulked her way through assembly.

And second, there was the unbelievable vision of Miss Ambler dressed to kill.

'She's wearing make-up!' Jade had sniggered as the teacher walked in to take registration.

'She's streaked her hair!' Winona whispered, stunned by the complete makeover. 'And that's a designer label shirt!'

'Look at those shoes; trendy or what!'

Maya spoke up from her corner at the back of the class.

'Never mind the shoes; what about the trousers?' Kyle pointed out the skin-tight pair clinging to Miss Ambler's legs.

New clothes, hair-dye, make-up, perfume – the full works for Louise. What had got into their mouse-like teacher?

'Would you like to know what the surprise is?' Ambler asked, teetering on her high heels, teasing them.

Yes - yes - yes! the whole class begged.

'Well, you all remember Nathan's cheeky remark about my famous boyfriend,' she began coyly.

'Yes, miss!' All the kids held their breaths.

Daisy could hear the cogs inside her brain slowly grinding and crunching. "Famous boyfriend"? But wasn't that purely the product of Daisy's own over-heated imagination? Hadn't she made it all up inside her head?

'As you know, I don't like to drag my personal life into school with me,' Miss

Ambler went on, 'but since Nathan somehow blew my cover, as you might say, I thought I might as well use my connections (*nudge-nudge, wink-wink*) to give you all a treat.'

'Wow! Cool! C'mon, Miss, tell us!'

Daisy glared at Jimmy, whose eyes had glazed over and whose grin had grown fixed on his pointed face.

'All in good time,' their newly-glamorous teacher assured them.

'Let's just say that it may have something to do with your favourite football team. Meanwhile, I'm enjoying keeping the secret.'

'Aw, Miss! Please, Miss!'

Her glossy lips smiled as she turned her head to look out of the window at a low, sporty silver car which had just swung into the playground. 'Look outside!' she whispered.

So they stood and craned their necks, Jimmy and Daisy along with all the rest.

They watched the gleaming doors open. They gasped once, then twice as two men stepped out of the car.

Daisy leaned forward to the desk in front to grab Jimmy's blue shirt. 'Did you set this up?' she hissed, her head in a complete spin.

Jimmy shook his head. 'Search me!'

The two men sauntered towards the entrance, hands in tracksuit pockets.

'Then, how...?' Daisy stuttered.

Jimmy tugged free and turned on her. 'Listen, I admit that I went behind your back to get the autographs!' he hissed. 'I couldn't resist; I just wanted to see your face when I brought them in.'

'Hmm. So how did you get them?'

'Easy. I went round to Bernie King's flat on Saturday lunchtime, knowing there was a benefit match between the firsts and the junior squad in the afternoon. So I asked Bernie if he would ask William to get the whole first team and the Steelers manager to give me their autographs. He told me, sure; anything for a genuine fan like me. It was as simple as that!'

'Jammy!' Daisy breathed. She gazed out of the window through narrowed eyes. 'But you're sure you didn't have anything to do with this?'

The buzz of excitement inside the classroom rose as the unexpected guests entered the building. Chairs scraped, kids crowded towards the door.

'Swear, cross my heart and hope to die!'
Jimmy insisted.

Major mystery.

Because it was Steelers manager, Kevin
Crowe, opening the door and walking into
the classroom.

And, behind him, with rays of sunlight
falling on his corn-stubble haircut and with a
shy grin on his handsome, square face was
Super-Rob, top goal-scorer in the
Premiership, national hero and demi-god.

'...Ohhhhhhhhhh!' the whole class gasped.

Miss Ambler smiled and went forward to
greet the star.

Robbie Exley smiled back. He embraced
the teacher and kissed her on the cheek.

Eight

Am I dreaming? Daisy stood with her mouth open. Robbie Exley had just kissed Miss Ambler.

OK, so it had only been on the cheek. But it *was* in front of the whole class.

The teacher smiled and embraced the soccer star.

Daisy blinked, then glanced at a gobsmacked Jimmy.

Weak at the knees, Jimmy sat down hard at his desk. 'ROB-BIE EX-LEY!' he mouthed, eyes shining, cheeks flushed.

Robbie and Kevin in their very own school, wearing flash Steelers tracksuits, windswept and glowing as if they'd come straight from the training ground.

The door opened again. Thirty two heads turned to see a tall blonde woman enter the room. Thin and tanned, with her hair pulled back and sprouting carelessly from a sparkly clasp, she glided towards Miss Ambler.

'Hey, Louise,' she said casually in a thick foreign accent.

Then she too hugged and kissed the teacher.

'Ingrid Salminen!' Wannabe Winona gasped, so loud that everybody heard. She noted every detail of the supermodel's styling so that she could go home and practise in the mirror later.

Help! a small voice inside Daisy's head cried.

What's going on?

Emerging from the elegant embrace, Miss Ambler smiled at the class. 'I take it that our visitors need no introduction. But in case anyone is still wondering, I'd like you to meet Ingrid Salminen and Robbie Exley.'

As she spoke, the two superstars linked up. Lovey-dovey, hands around waists, smiling warmly into each others' eyes.

No! Wait! Action replay! First Robbie was kissing and hugging Miss Ambler. Now he was making out that he and Ingrid were still an item. Daisy couldn't work it out.

'And this is my friend, Kevin Crowe,' Miss Ambler went on shyly. 'I'm sure you all recognise him from his appearances on "TV Sport".'

Kevin chose that moment to step forward from the shadow of Robbie and Ingrid's golden glory. He grinned at the rows of stunned faces. And then, unbelievably, he slipped his own arm around their teacher's waist.

'See, she *did* have a famous boyfriend!' Nathan pointed out in his smarmiest know-all voice.

The playtime bell had gone and a gaggle of kids from 5A were gathered around the gate from where they'd waved off their superstar visitors.

Robbie and Kevin had answered a load of eager questions and told funny stories about the world of soccer. Robbie had grinned sheepishly but refused to show the class his shoulder tattoo. Then, finally, the famous three had said goodbye.

'And thank you for making this a very special day at Woodbridge School!' Miss Ambler had spoken for everyone.

Ingrid and Robbie had signed autographs, while Kevin had chatted quietly with the teacher. He'd kissed her and given her a squeeze on the way out.

'No wonder she didn't deny it,' Winona added.

Definitely
96
Daisy

'Wasn't that mega mega mega mega mega mega cool!' Jimmy sighed, eeking out the last glimpse of the silver car as it slid around the corner. All the confusion and betrayal of the last few days had melted away in the glory of the moment.

'Daisy, wasn't that the coolest?'

'Yeah, cool,' she muttered, still reeling from the shock. No wonder Miss Ambler had glammed up for the occasion. If Kevin had seen her in her workaday cream blouse and blue skirt, he might well have changed his mind about going out with her!

And the teacher had scrubbed up well, Daisy had to admit.

But really, Nathan was a pain, going on about things the way he was.

'Only one problem,' he smirked. 'The famous boyfriend turns out NOT to be Robbie Exley, like Daisy claimed!'

The whole gang took in what Nathan said. They bunched up their mouths and narrowed their eyes.

'Hey, yeah!' Jared said slowly.

'How come?' Maya asked.

Winona stepped up close. 'Yeah, Daisy; how come?'

Frantically Daisy looked for an answer. She turned to Jimmy, who was still sighing and drooling over the visit. No help there. 'I must've read it wrong in Miss Ambler's diary,' she muttered weakly.

'Typical!' Nathan poured scorn on her excuse. He pushed his glasses more firmly on to his nose. 'Now, if you'd just bothered to read more carefully, you'd have soon seen that Miss Ambler was going out with Kevin Crowe. It's there in black and white.'

Flip-flop. Daisy's heart turned over. How could Nathan possibly know? Unless he'd ferreted around in Daisy's bag and discovered the secret black book. Wait a second; didn't she recall Nathan hanging about on the step by the main entrance earlier that morning? Yeah; he'd tripped over the bag just before she and Jared had run off to meet Jimmy. And, disaster - she'd left the bag on the step for anyone to rummage through...

Oh no! *Flip-flop-flap!* Daisy's stomach heaved and rolled as she silently split away from the gang and sped back into school.

Jimmy and Nathan followed more slowly with knowing looks.

'Daisy Morelli, get out!' Mrs Hunt waylaid her by the cloakroom. 'It's dry-play. You're not allowed in school!'

Daisy ducked around the corner and sped on. She'd have to face Moaning Minnie later, no doubt. But she needed to find her bag. It was a matter of life and death.

Zooming down the corridor, heart thumping and mouth dry, Daisy made it to the classroom. She flung open the door, then wove through rows of desks to reach her own.

There was her bag, hanging half-empty on the back of her chair. She ripped open its velcro fastening and delved inside. Her groping fingers made contact with her lunchbox, her pencil-case, a pair of dead socks...

'Daisy?' Miss Ambler asked from the stock-room door.

Daisy jumped back guiltily. No diary! Definitely no diary in the bag!

'Are you sure you're all right?' the teacher wiggled towards her on her high heels.

'Fine!' Daisy squeaked. Not only no diary, but no Herbie either! Both book and hamster were missing.

'You don't look well,' Miss Ambler insisted in a concerned voice. 'Has the excitement of the morning been too much?'

'Yes, Miss. I suppose so, Miss.' OK, so Nathan had snuck behind her back and stolen the diary. But what for? It didn't make any sense, unless, unless...

'Stop that dog!' Nathan's shout echoed down the corridor.

'Jimmy, grab that book from Lennox before he chews it to bits!'

Huff-huff-huff! Fat Lennox panted and pounded past the classroom.

Or at least, Miss Ambler and Daisy were meant to think he did.

Clicking into action while the teacher stood marooned in the middle of the room, Daisy dashed to the door in time to see not Lennox, but Jimmy crouching low and imitating the bulldog's wheeze. *Huff-huff! Grrraaggh!*

'Got it!' Jimmy growled, then held up the scruffy book.

'Well done!' Nathan congratulated him. 'Miss Ambler will be pleased that we've got her diary back!'

Huff-huff-huff... Jimmy pretended to be Lennox thundering off down the corridor.

'My diary?' Miss Ambler came up behind Daisy, in time to see Nathan and Jimmy hurrying in triumph towards her.

'Lennox had it all the time!' Nathan exclaimed with a sideways, smug look at Daisy. 'He must have grabbed it and run off with it after sports day. No wonder it looks so chewed up!'

'The dog ate Ambler's diary!' Jimmy

announced with a wide grin, back in the
playground before the end of break.

Things had happened fast and Daisy was
only just beginning to recover. The teacher
had been deeply grateful to Jimmy and
Nathan. Daisy herself was off the hook at last.

'Yeah, yeah!' Jade, Jared, Maya and
Winona smirked. 'Fat Lennox is innocent. Free
Fat Lennox!'

'Well, Ambler thinks he did,' Nathan
confirmed, 'and that's what matters.' Then he

turned to Daisy. 'No need to thank me!' he crowed.

'I wasn't going to...' she muttered.

'Anyway, I was acting under orders. I only sneaked the diary out of your bag and set up the Lennox trick because Jimmy told me to.'

Daisy turned slowly to her friend. 'Jimmy?'

He shrugged his skinny shoulders. 'Yeah, well, someone had to do something to help you out of the hole you'd got yourself into. And I knew if I involved Nathan, Ambler would believe anything he said.'

'Clever!' Winona nodded. 'Good thinking, Jim.'

The trick had sent Jimmy's reputation rocketing sky-high.

'And what about Herbie?' Daisy demanded, crossing her arms in a giant huff. 'Why did you have to nick him too?'

Jimmy rolled his eyes towards Nathan. He spread his hands palms upwards. 'I don't know what you're talking about!'

'Yes, you do! Herbie's gone missing. You

told Nathan to steal him!'

Jimmy's eyebrows shot up under his fringe, all innocent. 'Me?'

'Yes, you! To get your own back!'

Winona, Jared and the rest tuned in with fresh interest. A row between Jimmy and Daisy? This was something new.

'What for?' Jimmy pretended to be puzzled.

'You know!' For lying to him about the diary entry. But the others didn't know about that. And Jimmy knew that Daisy knew that they didn't know... Daisy got lost in the maze of pretence and gave up.

'I wouldn't worry about Herbie,' he teased, grinning at geeky Nathan. 'I guess he just went for a walk around school.'

'He's a stuffed toy!' Winona reminded everyone. She was a girl with no visible sense of humour. 'How can he wander off?'

Jimmy tossed his fringe back, shrugged, but said nothing.

Daisy fumed and fretted.

Serves you right! said Herbie, tucked
securely into Jimmy's waistband beneath the
oversized football shirt. Frankly, he refused to
lift a paw to help.

Jimmy grinned and practised a dodging
dribble around Daisy, his flat-footed
opponent. 'Herbie will show up,' he assured
her wickedly. 'All in his own good time!'

Look out for more Definitely Daisy
adventures - coming soon!

I'd like a little word, Leonie!

Jenny Oldfield

It's World Book Day and Daisy's class
dress up as book characters. Leonie's
really into it - until she sees nerdy Nathan
wearing the same outfit as her. But when
she messes up an important task for Miss
Boring-Snoring, Daisy twigs that their twin
cat costumes could be a way out of
trouble for golden girl, Leonie...

Not now, Nathan!

Jenny Oldfield

Nerdy Nathan's pet spider has gone missing. Daisy and the gang carry out a frantic search, but they fail to find crafty Legs. Poor Nathan's worried sick. But scatty Miss Ambler, busy rehearsing for Thursday's school concert, has no time to waste on a pesky runaway pet...